The Hair Washing Zorba

By Erik Ohlsen

Illustrations by Myriad Colorz

STORYSCAPES

For my children, Phoenix and Iyla

The Hair Washing Zorba
By Erik Ohlsen
Illustrations by Myriad Colorz

ISBN: 978-0-9975202-0-0

Published by StoryScapes
storyscapes.us
StoryScapes PO Box 116,
Sebastopol, CA 95473

info@storyscapes.us

STORYSCAPES

StoryScapes

At StoryScapes, we are inspired to create stories full of magic, environmental stewardship, family connections, cultural healing, and healthy living. Our goal is to support a thriving world through story telling. Stay up to date with our new releases, enjoy life, and love nature!

www.storyscapes.us

Get these new titles from StoryScapes:

The Living Playground
The Forest of Fire
The Hair Washing Zorba (ages 3-5)
This Farm's Life (Adult Coloring Book)
Our Living Earth (Adult Coloring Book)

Check out our sister companies:

Permaculture Skills Center LLC
www.permacultureskillscenter.org

Permaculture Artisans Contracting
www.permacultureartisans.com

ForeSite Mapping LLC
www.foresitemapping.com

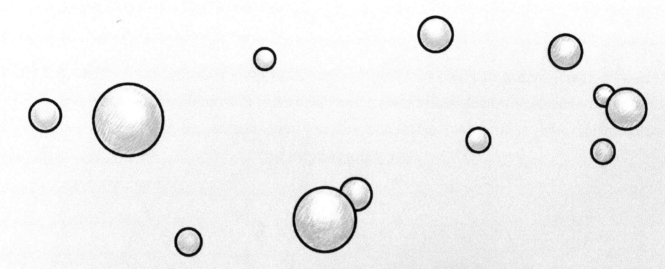

Sometimes it's hard to get your hair washed.
Your face gets all wet and your head gets all squashed.
You might thrash and splash with soapy hair strands.
This hair washing stuff can get out of hand!

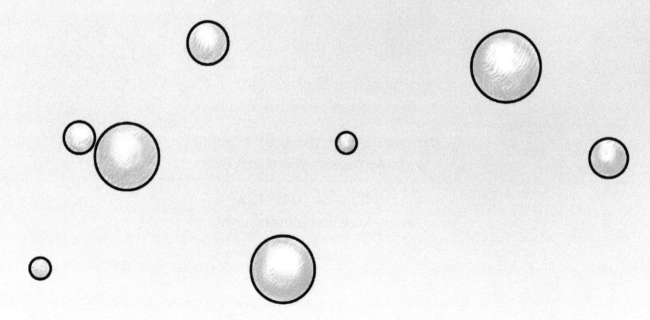

We have a solution, here comes a great cure!
Call hair washing Zorba for a plan that is sure.

You will have so much fun while he cleans up your muck.
His magic fills hair with adventure and luck.

Washing hair is fun when Zorba comes around.
Kids smile and clean without a single frown.
Zorba's tricks that he shares come from animal friends.

They have taught him of feathers and soft furry ends.
Oh, kids! Get ready, you'll love what comes next:
Zorba's fun hair styles. You choose which is best!

Your hair could be flowing like a great and grand horse,
As she gallops through meadows of grass, and jumps gorse.

Coyote hair is so much fun.
Joyfully you'll howl under the sun!

Chicken-style hair many kids do not dread.

For its light showy glamour looks nice on their head.

An Iguana-style frop may even feel cool.
Its mohawk of scales can be used as a tool.

The Peacock's fine plume will make you feel royal.
Through the forest you'll glide with all who are loyal.

With a giraffe hairdo you'll see from up high!
And a snack you may eat from large trees you pass by.
Do you still need more? Then what about this…

Zorba has many more styles on his list!
Like the great Rhino hair, so tall and horn-shaped,
You'll tromp through a place that's thickly landscaped.

How 'bout an Alpaca-do that you can strut,
With long shiny curls and soft bangs that are cut?

Or in golden rays you can bask, and roar, too
When Zorba makes Lion's Grand King hairdo.
There are so many options you get choose from.
You'll say to your parents, and you may even hum...

"We love washing our hair. It's just so much fun!"
Dear kids, our secret we're happy to share:
Make a game with your parents of washing your hair.

With a horse you may run. Like a bird you may fly.
And in case you get worried, Zorba's always close by…

About the Author

Erik Ohlsen

Looking back on his childhood, Erik fondly remembers family vacations spent exploring outside, hiking, camping, and swimming. This connection to and love of the natural world inspired his career as an ecological landscape and farm designer and committed community organizer. Dedicating his life to this work since 1998, he is now recognized internationally as a leader in these fields.

He is the Executive Director of the Permaculture Skills Center, a vocational training school in ecological design, landscaping, farming, and land stewardship.

Erik is the Owner/Principal at Permaculture Artisans, a fully licensed design/contracting firm specializing in ecological landscapes and farms.

He is also the Principal at ForeSite LLC digital mapping company and Founder/Author of the StoryScapes book series.

Erik resides in Sebastopol, California with his wife Lauren. Together they are raising a family, managing their homestead, and running their businesses.

Printed in the USA
CPSIA information can be obtained
at www.ICGtesting.com
CBHW061700251124
17970CB00043B/1096

9 780997 520200